A T L A S

ATLAS

by Jorge Luis Borges

In Collaboration with María Kodama

Translated and Annotated by Anthony Kerrigan

E. P. DUTTON / NEW YORK

Originally published in Argentina under the title *Atlas,* © 1984 Editorial Sudamericana S.A.

This English translation and Notes copyright © 1985 by Anthony Kerrigan.

Published in the United States by E. P. Dutton, a division of New American Library, 2 Park Avenue, New York, N.Y. 10016

Library of Congress Cataloging in Publication Data
Borges, Jorge Luis.
    Atlas.

    Translation of: Atlas.
    I. Kodama, María. II. Title.
PQ7797.B635A913   1985   910   85-13090

ISBN: 0-525-24344-5

Published simultaneously in Canada by Fitzhenry & Whiteside Limited, Toronto

W

10 9 8 7 6 5 4 3 2 1

FIRST EDITION

Contents

Prologue

I believe it was John Stuart Mill who first spoke of the plurality of causes. As regards this book—which is certainly not, by the by, an atlas—I am able to point to two causes, both unequivocal. The first one is called Alberto Girri, a leading Argentine poet. In the pleasant course of our residence on earth, María Kodama and I have traveled and savored many regions, and they have suggested many photographs and many pages of text. The second cause, the publisher and critic Enrique Pezzoni, saw them; Girri observed that they could be interwoven into a prudently chaotic book. Here is that book. It does not consist of a series of texts illustrated by photographs or a series of photographs explained by texts. Each section embodies a union of words and images. To discover the unknown is not a prerogative of Sinbad, of Eric the Red, or of Copernicus. Each and every man is a discoverer. He begins by discovering bitterness, saltiness, concavity, smoothness, harshness, the seven colors of the rainbow and the twenty-some letters of the alphabet; he goes on to visages, maps, animals and stars. He ends with doubt, or with faith, and the almost total certainty of his own ignorance.

María Kodama and I have shared the joy and surprise of finding sounds, languages, twilights, cities, gardens and people, all of them distinctly different and unique. These pages would wish to be monuments to that long adventure which still goes on.

J. L. B.

The Gallic Goddess

When Rome reached this ultimate terrain and its indefinite and perhaps endless freshwater sea, when Caesar and Rome, those two high and clarion names, arrived, the burnt-wood goddess was already here. They would have called her Diana or Minerva, in the indifferent manner of empires which are not missionary and prefer to recognize and annex vanquished deities. Previously she might have occupied a place in an exact hierarchy, have been the daughter of one god and the mother of another and associated with the outpourings of spring or the horrors of war. Now she is lodged, and exhibited, in that curious place, a museum. She comes to us without mythology, without a word of her own, with only the muted clamor of buried generations. She is a broken and sacred image which our idle imagination can inconsequentially enhance. We shall never hear the prayers of her worshippers, we shall never know her rites.

The Totem

Plotinus of Alexandria refused to allow a portrait to be made of himself, we are told by Porphyry, alleging that he was merely a shadow of his Platonic prototype and that a portrait would be the shadow of a shadow. Centuries later, Pascal rediscovered this argument against the art of painting. The image we see here is a photograph of a facsimile of an idol in Canada, that is: the shadow of a shadow of a shadow. Its original, so to say, stands, elevated but without a cult following, behind the last of the three rail stations in

Retiro. It is an official gift of the Canadian government. That country does not mind being identified with a barbarous image. No South American government would run the risk of being represented by the effigy of a crude anonymous divinity.

We know all these things and yet our imagination is taken with the notion of an exiled totem, a totem darkly demanding mythologies, tribes, incantations and even perhaps sacrifices. We know nothing of its cult following: one more reason to dream it in the equivocal twilight.

Caesar

Here lies what the daggers left.
Here lies that poor thing, a dead
man called Caesar. They cleft
craters in his flesh with their dread
metal. Here lies the atrociously stalled
machine, yesterday a vehicle of glory
for writing and making living history
and living it himself with full intent.
Here also lies the Other, the prudent
emperor who, declining laurel crowns to be free
for command on land or sea,
was honor and envy of all.
Here also still another, the future lord
whose great shadow will be the world.

Ireland

Ancient ample shades do not desire that I discern Ireland, or they do not want me to perceive it clearly in a historically sequential way. These shades bear such names as Scotus Erigena, for whom all our history is merely an extended dream of God's, one which eventually devolves on God, a doctrine which is declared in the drama *Back to Methuselah,* and the famous poem "Ce que dit la Bouche d'Ombre" of Hugo. The shades are also called George Berkeley, who judged that God is minutely dreaming us and that, if

He were to awake from His dream, heaven and earth would disappear—just as if the Red King were to awake. The shades are also called Oscar Wilde, who, from the depths of a fate not without misfortune and dishonor, left us a body of work as felicitous and innocent as water or dawn. I think of Wellington, who, after the feat at  Waterloo, felt that victory is no less terrible than defeat. I think of two great baroque poets, Yeats and Joyce, who used prose or verse to the same end, beauty. I think of George Moore, who created a new literary genre with *Ave Atque Vale,* a deed of little import but delightfully done, and that is no mean achievement. These vast shades interpose themselves between the great deal I remember and the little

I could garner in the course of two or three days, filled, like all days, with circumstance.

The most vivid of my impressions of Ireland in those few days was the Round Tower I did not see with my eyes but with my hands, a tower where, during hard times, the monks who are our benefactors saved Latin and Greek, that is, culture, for our inheritance. For me Ireland is a land of essentially benevolent and naturally Christian people carried away by the curious passion to be incessantly Irish.

I also walked the streets where all the inhabitants of *Ulysses* walked, and continue to walk.

Wolf

Furtive and gray in the final twilight
it leaves its traces on the banks
of the nameless river which slaked
the thirst of its gullet
with water repeating no stars.
Tonight the wolf is a lone shadow,
a form pursuing its mate, enduring cold.
It is the last wolf in England.
Thor and Odin know. A king
in his high stone house has sworn
to purge the country of wolves. The dire
iron of death has been forged.
Saxon wolf, you have bred in vain.
Cruelty is not enough. You are the last.
A thousand years afterward an old man
will dream you in America. This future
dream will do you no good.
The men who followed your traces
through the forest have surrounded you,
furtive and gray in the final twilight.

Istanbul

Carthage is the most notorious example of a defamed culture. We are unable to determine anything about "The City"; Flaubert could establish nothing about it—except from its enemies, who were implacable. It is perhaps not unlikely that something similar is happening as regards Turkey. We think of a cruel country. This notion dates from the Crusades, which were the most cruel enterprise in recorded history, and the least condemned. We think of Christian hatred, perhaps not inferior to equally fanatical Islamic hatred. In the West, we note the lack of a great Turkish name among these Ottomans. The sole name to remain with us is that of Suleiman the Magnificent (*e solo, in parte, vidi 'l Saladino*).

What can I know of Turkey at the end of three days? I have seen a splendid city and the Bosphorus and the Golden Horn and the entrance to the Black Sea, on whose shores runic stones have been discovered. I have heard an agreeable tongue, which sounds like a softer German. The shades of many and diverse nations must roam hereabouts: I choose to recall that the Scandinavians made up the honor guard of the Emperor of Byzantium, and that they were joined by the Saxons who fled England after the episode at Hastings. Doubtless we should return to Turkey to begin its discovery.

Gifts

To him was given invisible music,
a gift of time, which in time will halt.
Beauty was given him, a beauty tragic.
Love was given him, most terrible gift of all.

To him was given knowledge that the beauties
of women in the world numbered only one.
A certain afternoon he perceived
the moon, and with it the algebra of stars.

To him was given infamy. With meekness
he studied the crimes of the sword,
the ruins of Carthage,
the close struggle between East and West.

To him was given language, that lie.
To him was given flesh, which is dust.
To him was given a nightmare of disgust.
And mirrored in the glass, the Other, holding us in his eye.

Among the books which time has amassed,
a few pages were conceded him;
from Elea a store of paradox,
spared from time's eroding blast.

The heightened blood of human love
(the image was coined by a Greek) was his award
from the One whose name is a sword,
and who hands down literature from above.

Other things were given, each with its name:
the cube, the sphere, the pyramid,
innumerable sands, wood,
and for walking among men, a bodily frame.

He deserved the savor of each day's time:
such is your history, as it is also mine.

Venice

The artificers were: the rugged rocks, the rivers whose source is in the summits, the fusion of the waters of these rivers with those of the Adriatic Sea, the chance or fatality of history and geology, the tides, the sands, the gradual formation of the islands, the proximity of Greece, the fish, the migration of the folk, the Armorican and Baltic wars, the reed huts, the branches held together with mud, the inextricable network of canals, the primitive wolves, the incursions of Dalmatian pirates, the delicacy of terra-cotta, the flat-roofed terraces, the marble, Attila's horse herds and lances, the fisherfolk protected by their poverty, the Lombards, the fact that this is a place where the East and West meet, the days and nights of long-forgotten generations. Let us also recall the gold rings the Doge let fall each year from the bow of the galley *Bucentaurus:* in the penumbra, in the obscurity of the water these are the indefinite links in an ideal chain of time. It would be an injustice to fail to mention here the solicitous searcher for the Aspern Papers, or Dandolo, or Carpaccio, or Petrarch, or Shy-

lock, or Byron, or Beppo, or Ruskin or Proust. High in one's memory are the bronze captains who have been watching each other invisibly all these centuries from the two ends of an extended plain.

Gibbon observes that the independence of the ancient republic of Venice was declared by the sword and may be justified by the pen. Pascal writes that rivers are highways that travel: the canals of Venice are highways down which travel gondolas wearing mourning, gondolas like mourning violins, melodious gondolas that remind us of music.

In some prologue I remember writing the phrase *crystal and crepuscular Venice*. Twilight and Venice are for me practically synonymous words. Twilight for us has lost its light and is fearful of nightfall, while the twilight of Venice is delicate and eternal, without a before or an after.

Bollini's Alley

As contemporaries of the revolver, of the rifle, of mysterious atomic weapons, of vast world wars, of the conflicts in Vietnam and Lebanon, we can only feel nostalgia for the modest, secret battles waged in this place around the 1890s a few steps from the Rivadavia Hospital. The area between the back of the cemetery and the yellow walls of the prison was at one time called Tierra del Fuego. The slumdwellers, we are told, chose that alley, Bollini's shortcut, for their knife fights or duels. Perhaps there was only one knife fight and later there was talk of many. There were no witnesses except, perhaps, some curious policeman, who would have appreciatively observed the comings and goings of the steel blades. A poncho thrown over the left arm would have served as shield. The knife point would have been searching for the belly or breast of the opponent. If the duelists were dexterous, the combat might be prolonged.

Whatever the case, it is gratifying to be inside this house at nightfall, under the high ceilings, and know that the remaining low houses outside still stand amid the memory of the long-gone tenement corrals teeming with the doubtless apocryphal shades of this barren mythology.

The Temple of Poseidon

I suspect that there *was* no God of the Sea, nor a God of the Sun: both concepts are alien to the primitive mind. There was simply the sea, and there was Poseidon, who was also the sea. The theogonies and Homer came much later. According to Samuel Butler, Homer simply wove subsequent tales around the comic interludes in the *Iliad*. Time and its wars have carried away the likeness of the God, but there is still the sea, his other effigy.

My sister is fond of saying that children antecede Christianity. Despite their cupolas and icons, so do the Greeks. In any case, their religion was less a discipline than a complex of dreams, whose divinities are less powerful than the Great God Ker. The temple of Poseidon dates from the fifth century before our era, that is, before the philosophers put everything in doubt.

There is nothing in the world that is not mysterious, but the mystery is more evident in certain things than in others: in the sea, in the eyes of the elders, in the color yellow and in music.

The Beginning

Two Greeks converse: perhaps Socrates and Parmenides.

It is best if we never know their names; in that way, the story will be simpler and more mysterious.

The theme of the dialogue is abstract. They sometimes allude to myths, in which they both disbelieve.

The reasons they allege may abound in fallacies and they do not come to a conclusion.

They do not polemicize. And they do not want to persuade or be persuaded: they do not think in terms of winning or losing.

They are in agreement on a single point: they know that discussion is the not-impossible way to find a truth.

Free of myth and metaphor, they think or attempt to think.

We shall never know their names.

This conversation between two unknowns someplace in Greece is the capital event in History.

They have forgotten prayer and magic.

Voyage in a Balloon

As dreams demonstrate, as the angels demonstrate, flying is one of the elemental anxieties of man. Levitation has not yet been given me and there is no reason whatever to suppose I will experience it before I die. Aircraft certainly do not provide us with anything resembling the feeling of flight. The sensation of being locked in an ordered enclosure of glass and metal is not comparable to the flight of birds or of angels. The terrifying predictions of the cabin crew with their ominous enumeration of oxygen masks, safety belts, lateral exit doors and the impossible aerial acrobatics are not, nor can be, auspicious. The clouds cover and dissemble continents and seas. The trajectory borders on tedium. A balloon, on the other hand, gives us the conviction of flight, the agitation of a neighborly wind, the proximity of birds. Every word presupposes a shared experience. If someone has never seen the color red, it is useless for me to compare it with the blooded moon of St. John the Theologian, or with wrath. If a person is ignorant of the felicity of a trip in a balloon, it is difficult for me to

30

BALLOON AVIATION
OF NAPA VALLEY

explain it. I have used the word *felicity:* I believe it is the most adequate. Some thirty days ago, in California, María Kodama and I went to a modest building somewhere in the Napa Valley. It must have been about four or five o'clock in the morning: we knew that the first light of day would soon be upon us. A truck carried us to an even more distant place, with the balloon basket in a trailer behind us. We arrived at a site which could have been anywhere on the plain. They unloaded the basket, a wood and wicker rectangle, and carefully worked the large balloon out of its container; then they spread it on the ground, separated the nylon fabric. As it was inflated, the globe,

now in the form of an inverted pear, as shown in the encyclopedias of our youth, increased in size unhurriedly until it reached the height and width of a house several stories high. There was no side door or staircase to be seen: I was hoisted aboard. We were five passengers in all, plus the pilot, who periodically pumped gas into the great concave globe. Standing, we took hold of the basket's sides. As day came on, we beheld, at our feet, from the height of the angels or of high-flying birds, the vineyards and fields.

Space seemed unobstructed, and the unhurried wind, which carried us along as on a slow river, caressed our foreheads, our cheeks, the backs of our necks. I believe we all felt the same felicity, a felicity almost physical. I say *almost,* for there is no happiness or pain which is solely physical; the past always interposes itself, as do the circumstances, surprise and other ingredients of consciousness. The excursion, which must have lasted an hour and a half, was also a voyage through the lost paradise that is the nineteenth century. To travel in the balloon dreamed up by Montgolfier was to return to the pages of Poe, of Jules Verne, of Wells. It will be remembered that the "Selenites" who inhabited the interior of the moon traveled from one gallery to another in balloons similar to ours—and felt no vertigo.

A Dream in Germany

Early this morning I dreamed a dream which left me confounded; only later could I put it in some order.

Your forebears engender you.

On the far frontier of the deserts stand dusty classrooms or, if one prefers, dusty storerooms, with parallel rows of worn-out blackboards whose length is measured in leagues, or in leagues of leagues. The precise number of storerooms is not known; doubtless they are many. In each one there are nineteen rows of blackboards and someone has covered them with words and with Arabic numerals written in chalk. The door to each classroom is a sliding door, in the Japanese manner, and made of rusted metal. The writing starts on the left-hand margin of the blackboard and begins with a word. Under it is another and they all follow the strict alphabetic order of encyclopedic dictionaries. The first word is, let us say, *Aachen,* the name of a city. The second, immediately below it, is *Aare,* the river of Bern. In third place is *Aaron,* of the tribe of Levi. Then come *abracadabra,* and *Abraxas*.

After each one of these words is affixed the precise number of times you will see, hear, remember or use it during the course of your life. The number of times you will pronounce, between the cradle and the grave, the name of Shakespeare or of Kepler, is indefinite, but certainly not infinite. On the last blackboard in a remote classroom is the word *Zwitter*, German for hermaphrodite, and under it you will use up the number of images of the city of Montevideo which has been assigned to you by destiny, and you will go on living. You will use up the number of times assigned to you to articulate this or that hexameter, and you will go on living. You will use up the number of times your heart has been assigned a heartbeat, and then you will have died.

When this happens the chalk letters and numbers will not immediately be erased. (In each instant of your life someone modifies or erases a figure.) All this serves a purpose we will never understand.

Athens

On the first morning, my first day in Athens, I was proffered the following dream. In front of me stood a row of books filling a long shelf. They formed a set of the *Encyclopaedia Britannica,* one of my lost paradises. I took down a volume at random. I looked up Coleridge: the article had an end but no beginning. I looked up Crete: it concluded but did not begin. I looked up the entry on Chess. At that point the dream shifted. On an elevated stage in an amphitheater filled to capacity with an attentive audience, I was playing chess with my father, who was also the False Artaxerxes. (His ears having been cut off, Artaxerxes was found sleeping by one of his many wives; she ran her hand over his skull very gently so as not to awaken him; presently he was killed.) I moved a piece; my antagonist did not move anything but, by an act of magic, he erased one of my pieces. This procedure was repeated various times.

I awoke and told myself: *I am in Greece, where everything began, assuming that things, as opposed to articles in the dream's encyclopedia, have a beginning.*

Geneva

Of all the cities on this planet, of all the diverse and intimate places which a man seeks out and merits in the course of his voyages, Geneva strikes me as the most propitious for happiness. Beginning in 1914, I owe it the revelation of French, of Latin, of German, of Expressionism, of Schopenhauer, of the doctrine of Buddha, of Taoism, of Conrad, of Lafcadio Hearn and of the nostalgia of Buenos Aires. Also: the revelation of love, of friendship, of humiliation and of the temptation to suicide. In memory, everything is gratifying, even mischance. These reasons are personal. I'll cite one that is of a general order. Unlike other cities, Geneva is not emphatic. Paris does not ignore that it is Paris, decorous London knows that it is London. But Geneva scarcely knows that it is Geneva. The great shades of Calvin, of Rousseau, of Amiel, of Ferdinand Hodler are here, but no one recalls them to the traveler. A little like Japan, Geneva has renewed itself without losing its yesterdays. The small mountainous streets of the Vieille Ville, the bells and the fountains remain, but there also exists another great city of bookshops and East-West trade.

I know that I will always return to Geneva, perhaps after the death of my body.

The Corner of Piedras and Chile

I must have passed, and repassed, this place.
I no longer can recall. More distant
than the Ganges are the mornings
or afternoons I came by. The reversals
of fortune no longer count. They are part
of that malleable clay, my past,
which erases time or is subsumed to art,
no part of it announced by any augur.
Perhaps a sword gleamed in the mists,
or perhaps it was a rose. Interwoven
shadows now conceal them in their sheaths.
Nothing remains but their ashes. Nothing.
Absolved of all the masks I've worn
in death I'll come to be oblivion.

The Brioche

The Chinese believe—some Chinese believe and continue to believe—that every new thing on earth projects its archetype to heaven. Someone or Something at present possesses the archetype of the sword, the archetype of the table, the archetype of the Pindaric Ode, the archetype of the syllogism, the archetype of the sand-clock, the archetype of the watch, the archetype of the map, the archetype of the telescope, the archetype of the scale. Spinoza observed that everything longs to endure in its being: the tiger wants to be a tiger, the stone, a stone. Personally, I have observed that there is nothing that does not show a tendency to be its own archetype—and sometimes is. One need only be in love to think that the other one is his or her own archetype. María Kodama got this grand brioche at the bakery Aux Brioches de la Lune, and she told me, when she brought it to the hotel, that it was the Archetype. I understood immediately. Let the reader look at its image and judge.

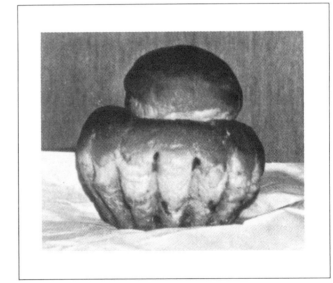

A Monument

It is legitimate to assume that a sculptor may set out in search of a subject, even though this mental version of the hunt is less proper for an artist than it would be for a man in pursuit of surprises. It would seem more likely to conjecture that the eventual artist is simply a man who suddenly sees in a flash. One need not be blind or have one's eyes closed in order not to see: we see what we've committed to memory, just as we *think* whatever it is we've committed to memory when we repeat identical ideas or forms. I am quite sure that Mr. So-and-So, "whose name I can no longer recall," saw something at a glance that no one had ever seen before since the beginning of history. What he saw was a button. He saw that everyday artifact which so engages the fingers and he understood that in order to transmit this disclosure, the revelation of something so simple, he must augment its size and execute the vast and serene circle we see on the facing page and at the center of a square in Philadelphia.

43

Epidaurus

Like someone viewing a battle from afar, like someone scenting the salt air and hearing the work of the waves and sensing the sea, like someone entering a country or a book, I attended a performance of *Prometheus Bound* in the high theater of Epidaurus the night before last. My ignorance of Greek is as perfect as Shakespeare's, except in the case of the numerous Hellenic words which designate devices or disciplines unknown to the Greeks. At first I attempted to remember Spanish versions of the tragedy, translations I had read more than a half-century before. Later I thought of Hugo and Shelley, and then of an etching depicting the Titan bound to the mountain. Next I strove to identify some word or other. I thought of the myth that is part of the universal memory of man. Without intending or anticipating it, I was carried away by the two musics, that of the instruments and that of the

words, whose sense was denied me, but not their ancient passion. Beyond the verses—which the actors, I believe, were not scanning, and the illustrious fable—that deep river in the deep night became mine.

Lugano

Alongside the words I am now dictating, there will be, I believe, the image of a great Mediterranean lake bordered by long, *lento,* mountains and the reflection in reverse of these same mountains in the lake. That is my sure recollection of Lugano. But there are others.

One of them is of a morning, not overly cold, in November 1918, when my father and I read on a slate board in an almost deserted plaza the chalk words announcing the surrender of the Central Empires, that is: the desired peace. We returned to the hotel and broke the good news (there was no radiotelephone as yet) and drank toasts, not of champagne but of Italian red.

I harbor other memories of Lugano, less important for world history than for my personal history. The first of these was my discovery of Coleridge's most famous ballad. I penetrated this silent sea of meter and image which Coleridge dreamt in the last years of the eighteenth century, before he saw the sea itself, which would disappoint him many years later when he went to Germany, since the sea of mere reality is less vast than Coleridge's Platonic sea. The second (except that there is no second, for the two are more or less simultaneous) was the revelation of another no less magical music, Verlaine's verse.

My Last Tiger

There have always been tigers in my life. Reading has been so inter-woven with all the other habits of my days that I really don't know if my first tiger was the one in a book engraving, or that other one, long dead, whose stubborn coming and going around the cage I watched in fascination from the opposite side of the iron bars. My father was fond of encyclopedias; I judged them, I'm sure, according to their pictures of tigers. I remember those reproduced by Montaner y Simón (a Bengal tiger and a white Siberian), and a separate one, a

studious pen drawing in which there was the suggestion of a river. These visual tigers were soon joined by those made of words: Blake's famous bonfire ("Tyger, tyger, burning bright") and Chesterton's definition: "An emblem of terrible elegance." When as a child I read the *Jungle Books* I was pained to find that Shere Khan was the villain of the fable rather than the friend of the hero. I would like to recall, but cannot, a sinuous tiger in a brush drawing by a Chinese who never saw a tiger but doubtless had seen the tiger's archetype. That Platonic tiger can be found in Anita Berry's *Art for Children*. One may well ask: why tigers and not leopards or jaguars? I can only answer that spots displease me while stripes do not. If I were to write *leopard* instead of tiger, the reader would at once intuit that I was prevaricating. To these visual and verbal tigers I have added another revealed to me by our friend Cuttini in that curious zoological garden called Mundo Animal, where they forego prison cells.

This tiger is of flesh and blood, and I arrived in its presence in a state of fearful felicity; its tongue licked my face and its indifferent or loving claw lingered atop my head. Unlike its precursors, this tiger was possessed of weight and odor.

I will not say that this astonishing tiger—it astonished me—is more real than the others, for an oak is no more real than the forms in a dream, but I would like to give thanks here to our friend, that flesh and blood tiger which my senses perceived that morning and whose image comes back to me in the same way as do the images of the tigers in books.

Midgarthormr

*Sea without end. Fish without
end. Green enclosing cosmogonic serpent—
green serpent and green sea—
the earth encircled. The serpent's mouth
bites its tail, though it comes from afar,
from the nether confine. The stern
ring pressing us is a tempest's splendor,
reflections of reflections, shadow and murmur.
It is also the amphisbaena. Its many eyes gaze
eternally one upon another, in an absence
of horror. Each head grossly scents
the irons of war and its spoils.
It was dreamed in Iceland. The gaping seas
have witnessed it and trembled.
It will return with the cursed
ship armed with dead men's nails.
Its inconceivable shadow will loom
high above the pale world on the day
of high wolves and splendid agony
of a twilight without name.
Its imaginary image darkens the air.
Toward dawn I saw it all in nightmare.*

Nightmare

I closed the door to my apartment and walked to the elevator. I was about to press the call button when a truly startling person arrested my attention. He was so tall that I should have understood that I was dreaming him. His stature was increased by a cone-shaped cap. His face (which I never saw in profile) had about it something of the Tatar, or what I imagine a Tatar to be, and it ended in a black beard, also cone shaped. His eyes gazed at me in a mocking manner. He was dressed in a long overcoat, black and glossy, covered with large white discs. It reached nearly to the floor. With a suspicion that perhaps I was dreaming, I ventured to ask him, in some language or other, why he was dressed in such a fashion. He gave me an ironic smile and unbuttoned his overcoat. I saw that under it was a long one-piece suit in the same material and covered with the same white discs, and I realized (in the way one does in dreams) that under it there would be another one.

At that exact moment I tasted the unmistakable savor of nightmare, and awoke.

Robert Graves at Deyá

As I write these lines, perhaps even as you read them, Robert Graves, beyond time and free of its dates and numbers, is dying in Mallorca. He is in the throes of death but not agonizing, for agony implies struggle. Nothing further from struggle and closer to ecstasy than that seated old man surrounded in his immobility by his wife, children and grandchildren, the youngest on his knee, and a variety of pilgrims from different parts of the world (one of them a Persian, I believe). The tall body continued faithful to its functions, though he did not see or hear or utter a word: his was a soul alone. I thought he could not make us out, but when I said goodbye he shook my hand and kissed María Kodama's hand. At the garden gate his wife said: "You must

51

come back! This is heaven!'' That was in 1981. We went back in 1982. His wife was feeding him with a spoon; everyone was sad and awaited the end. I am aware that these dates are, for him, a single eternal instant.

The reader will not have forgotten *The White Goddess*; I will recall here the gist of one of Graves's own poems.

Alexander did not die in Babylon at the age of thirty-two. After a battle he becomes lost and for many nights makes his way through the wilderness. Finally he descries the campfires of a bivouac. Yellow,

slant-eyed men take him in, succor him, and finally enlist him in their army. Faithful to his lot as a soldier, he serves in long campaigns across deserts which form part of a geography unknown to him. A day arrives on which the troop is paid off. He recognizes his own profile on a silver coin and says to himself: *This is from the medal I had struck to celebrate the victory at Arbela when I was Alexander of Macedon.*

This fable deserves to be very ancient.

Dreams

My physical body may be in Lucerne, in Colorado or in Cairo, but each morning when I awake, when I once again take on the habit of being Borges, I invariably emerge from a dream which takes place in Buenos Aires. Whether the dream-images involve sierras, or swamps with stilt huts, spiral staircases sunk in cellars, sand dunes whose grains of sand I must perforce count, all of them are a particular cross street in Buenos Aires: in the Palermo or Sur quarter. When I am sleepless I am always at the center of a vague luminous haze, gray or blue in hue. Asleep, in my dreams, I see or converse with the dead. None of these things surprises me in the least. I never dream in the present but only of a past-tense Buenos Aires, and of the galleries and skylights of the National Library on Mexico Street. Does all this mean that beyond the limits of my will and consciousness I am, irreparably, incomprehensibly, a *porteño*, a native-born descendant of the people of the port of Buenos Aires?

Corners

This surely is the image of any corner whatever in Buenos Aires. There's no need to tell me which. It could be the corner of Charcas and Maipú, where my own house is situated; I imagine it crowded with my own phantoms, inextricably bound in their comings and goings, crisscrossing each other's paths.

It could be the corner across the street, where today there is a tall edifice with ramps, and before that an elongated rooming house with flowerpots on the balcony, and before that a house of which I know nothing and, in the time of the dictator Rosas, an adobe edifice with a brick pavement on a dirt street. It could be the corner by that garden which was your paradise. It could be the corner by a

56

confectionery shop in Once, where Macedonio Fernández, so fearful of death, explained to us that dying is the most trivial thing that can befall us. It could be the one by the Almagro Sur library, where Léon Bloy was revealed to me. It could be the corner of a square not yet re-formed into an octagon, one of few that remain. It could be the corner by the house to which María Kodama and I brought a wicker basket bearing a slight Abyssinian kitten that was called Odin and had crossed the ocean. It could be the corner with a tree that will never know it is a tree and which is prodigal with its shade. It could be one of the many seen by Leandro Alem, before the closed carriage and the pistol shot that sufficed. It could be the one by the library where I discovered, in the course of time, two histories of Chinese philosophy. It could be the corner of Esmeralda and Lavelle, where Estanislao del Campo died. It could be each one of those that go to make up the scattered chessboard. It could be almost all of them and thus is the unseen archetype.

The Ship

It is a thing of wood, broken wood. It does not know, can never know, that it was premeditated and carved by men of the race of Brennus, who hurled his iron sword (in the terms preferred by legend) into the scales where the tribute-gold was being weighed and uttered the words *Vae Victis!* (which are also of iron). It must have had hundreds of sister ships, all of them now dust. It does not know, can never know, that it plied the waters of the Rhone and the Arve and that great freshwater sea, Lake Geneva, which dilates in the center of Europe. It does not know, can never know, that it plied another river, more ancient and incessant than any other and which is called Time. The Gauls carved it for that long voyage a century before Caesar, and it was exhumed in the middle of the nineteenth century at the crossing of two streets in the city. And now, without its knowledge, it is exhibited before our eyes and to our astonishment in a museum not far from the cathedral in which John Calvin preached predestination.

Hotel Esja, Reykjavik

The most modest things in life are often a kind of boon. I had just arrived at the hotel. I was, as always, in the middle of that clear haze visible to the eyes of the blind, and I set about exploring the undefined room which had been assigned me. Feeling my way along the walls, which were rather uneven, and circling the furniture, I discovered a large round column. It was so wide I could scarcely encompass it and had trouble getting my hands to meet behind it. I knew at once it was white. Firm and massive, it rose toward the ceiling. For some seconds I experienced the curious happiness one derives from a thing that is almost an archetype. I know that at that moment I recovered the elemental joy I first felt when the pure forms of Euclidean geometry—the cylinder, the cube, the sphere, the pyramid—were revealed to me.

59

The Labyrinth

This is the labyrinth of Crete. This is the labyrinth of Crete whose center was the Minotaur. This is the labyrinth of Crete whose center was the Minotaur that Dante imagined as a bull with a man's head in whose stone net so many generations were as lost as María Kodama and I were lost. This is the labyrinth of Crete whose center was the Minotaur that Dante imagined as a bull with a man's head in whose stone net so many generations were as lost as María Kodama and I were lost that morning, and remain lost in time, that other labyrinth.

Fountains

Among so many other things, Leopoldo Lugones has left us these staunch verses:

As a mountain-man I know the worth of the amity of stone for a soul.

How much of a mountain-man Lugones could claim to be I don't know, but the matter is one of merely geographical moment, and calling himself a mountain-man is less important than the aesthetic content of the epithet itself.

The poet declares the benign relationship, the amity between man

and stone. I wish to mention another, more essential, more mysterious relationship: that between man and water. It is more essential because we are made, not of flesh and blood, but of time, of evanescence, whose most immediate metaphor is water. Heraclitus pointed it out.

There are fountains in all manner of cities, but they have different reasons for existence. Among Mohammedan Arabic nations they are the product of an ancient desert nostalgia; the poets, as we know, sang of oases and reservoirs of water. In Italy fountains appear to satisfy the need for beauty typical of the Italian soul. In Switzerland we might say that the cities want always to be in the Alps, and that the numerous public fountains endeavor to echo the mountain cascades. In Buenos Aires they are more ornamental and more visible than in Geneva or Basel.

The Islands of Tigre

No other city I know borders on a secret archipelago of green islands which recede and disappear into the equivocal waters of a river so slow that literature has called it immobile. On one of these islands, one I've never seen, Leopoldo Lugones killed himself. He may have felt, perhaps for the first time in his life, that he was freeing himself, at last, of the mysterious duty of searching out metaphors, adjectives and verbs for everything in the world.

Many years ago, El Tigre supplied me images, probably all erroneous, to illustrate the Malay and African passages in Conrad's stories. These images will serve to erect a monument, doubtless less durable than the bronze of certain infinite Sundays. I recall Horace, who continues to be for me the most mysterious of poets, inasmuch as his stanzas cease but do not conclude, and are thus unconnected. It is not unlikely that his classic mind deliberately abstained from emphasis. I reread the above and confirm the fact—with a certain bittersweet melancholy—that everything in the world brings me back to a quotation or a book.

The Knife's Milonga

It came to me at Pehuajó
from some generous hands.
It is better not to know
the return of Rosas' bands.

On the leather and wood no mark
of the rood lies on its haft.
With dreams tiger dark
the steel dreams its tiger craft.

The knife dreams of a hand
to deliver it from oblivion.
But all depends on what the man
with the hand decides.

The Pehuajó dagger owes
not a single death.
For a tremendous
fate the forger forged its breadth.

Beholding it I can only foresee
a future filled with daggers
as well as swords and sabers
and other deadly forms

so many that the world draws
near the point of death,
so many that death knows
not which to choose.

Dream your easy dream
in this tranquil state.
Be not impatient, blade,
Rosas returns to his estate.

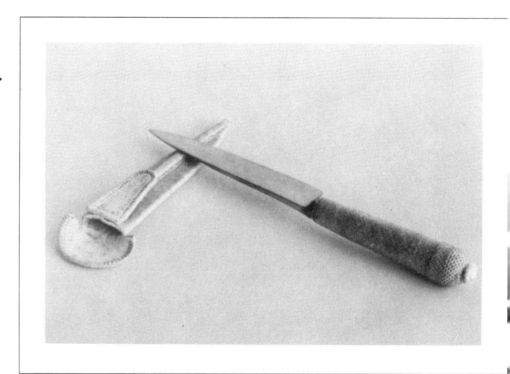

1983

Haydée Lange and I were conversing in a restaurant in the center of town. The table was still laid and there were a few crumbs and perhaps a couple of wineglasses. It is most likely to assume that we had just dined together. We were discussing, I believe, a film by King Vidor. There would have been a bit of wine left in the glasses. I felt, with the beginnings of boredom, that I was repeating myself, saying things I had said before and that she knew this and was answering me mechanically. All of a sudden, I remembered that Haydée Lange had died a long time ago. She was a ghost and didn't know it. I felt no fear, but felt it would not be right, and perhaps rude, to reveal to her that she was a ghost, a lovely ghost.

This dream branched out into another dream before I awoke.

Note Dictated from a Hotel in the Quartier Latin

Oscar Wilde writes that man is, at every instant of his life, everything he has been and everything he will be. If such is the case, the Wilde of the good years and good writing was already the Wilde of the gaol-house, the Wilde at Oxford, and the Wilde in Athens, and the one who would die in 1900, almost anonymously, in the Hôtel d'Alsace in the Latin Quarter. This hotel is now the Hotel l'Hôtel, where no two rooms are alike. One would think the place had been built by a cabinetmaker, rather than erected by masons, or according to an architect's design. Wilde despised realism, and the pilgrims who visit this sanctuary attest to its being redone as if it were a posthumous creation of Wilde's imagination.

I wanted to know the other side of the garden, Wilde told André Gide in his last years. No one is unaware that he knew infamy and prison, but there was in him something youthful and divine which rejected these misfortunes, and a certain famous ballad, which attempts the pathetic note, is not the most admirable of his works. I would say the same of his *The Picture of Dorian Gray,* a vain and lavish rewriting of the renowned novel by Robert Louis Stevenson.

What is the final savor left us by the works of Oscar Wilde? The mysterious savor of bliss. We think of champagne, that other fete. We recall with joy and gratitude "The Harlot's House," "The Sphinx," the aesthetic dialogues, the essays, the fairy tales, the epigrams, the lapidary bibliographic notes and the unending comedies that provide us with a host of stupid characters who are quite ingenious.

Wilde's style was in the decorative mode of a certain literary sect of his time, that of the Yellow Nineties, which sought visual and musical effects. He practiced this style, not without a smile, as he would have practiced any other style whatever.

A technical criticism of Wilde is beyond me. To think of him is to think of an intimate friend, one we have never seen but whose voice we know and every day miss.

Ars Magna

I am standing on the corner of Raymundo Lulio Street in Mallorca.

Emerson said that language is fossil poetry. As confirmation of this dictum, we need only remember that all abstract words are, in effect, metaphors, including the word *metaphor,* which in Greek means "transfer."

The thirteenth century, which professed the cult of Scripture—that is, of a set of words selected and approved by the Spirit—could not think in a metaphorical manner. A man of genius, Raymundo Lulio (Llull), who had attributed several definite predicates to God (goodness, greatness, eternity, power, wisdom, will, virtue and glory), conceived a sort of machine-for-thinking made up of concentric circles in wood covered with symbols of the divine predicates. This mechanism, set in motion by the systematic investigator, would yield an indefinite and almost

infinite number of concepts of a theological order. He did the same as regards the faculties of the soul and the qualities of everything in the world. As was to be expected, all these combinatory mechanisms served no purpose whatsoever.

Centuries later, Jonathan Swift mocked Llull in his *Third Voyage of Gulliver*. Leibniz considered the matter but abstained, naturally, from reconstructing the method.

The experimental science prophesied by Francis Bacon has now given us cybernetics, which has allowed man to set foot on the moon and whose computers are—if the phrase is acceptable—belated sisters of Llull's ambitious circles.

Mauthner observes that a dictionary of rhymes is also a machine-for-thinking.

La Jonction

Two rivers—one clearly famous, the Rhone; the other almost a secret, the Arve—here join forces. Mythology is not a vanity out of dictionaries, but an eternal habit of the spirit. Two rivers coming together are, in some measure, like two ancient numina which fuse. So Lavardén must have felt when he composed his ode; but rhetoric interposed itself between what he felt and what he saw, and converted the two great baroque rivers into mother-of-pearl. Apart from this, everything having to do with water is poetic and never ceases to disquiet us. The sea entering into the land becomes a fjord or firth, words of infinite  resonance. The rivers which are lost in the sea evoke Manrique's grand metaphor.

On these banks were buried the mortal remains of my maternal grandmother, Leonor Suárez de Acevedo. She had been born in Mercedes, Uruguay, during the small war still called there the Great War, and died in Geneva, Switzerland, around 1917. She lived on the memory of an equestrian feat performed by her father on the high pampa of Junín, and on hate, hate grown weary and become purely verbal, which she felt for "the three great tyrants of the River Plate: Rosas, Artigas and Solano López." She died exhausted. We all surrounded her bed, and she said, in a thin shred of a voice: "Let me die in peace," and then the indecent word that, for the first and last time, I heard from her mouth.

Madrid, July 1982

Space may be measured in *varas,* yards or kilometers. Time, as life span, does not fit into analogous measurements.

I have just suffered a first-degree burn. The doctor tells me that I must remain for ten or twelve days in this impersonal room in a Madrid hotel. I know that this given sum of days is an impossibility: I know that each day is made up of instants, which are the only reality, and that each instant will have its own savor of melancholy, of joy, of exaltation, of tedium, of passion. In some verse of his Prophetic Books, William Blake asserted that each minute consists of sixty-some gold palaces with sixty-some iron doors. This quotation is

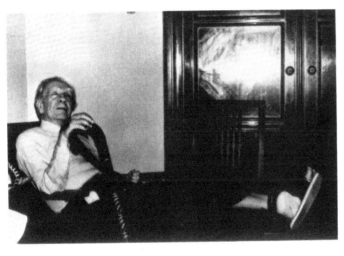

doubtless as hazardous and erroneous as the original. In a parallel way, Joyce's *Ulysses* summarizes the long adventures of the *Odyssey* within a single Dublin day, deliberately trivial.

My foot is a bit far from me, and sends me notices which seem like pain and are not pain. I already feel the nostalgia of that moment in which I shall feel nostalgia for this moment. In memory, the improbable time of this enforced stay will form one single image. I know I shall miss that memory when I am back in Buenos Aires. Perhaps tonight will be terrible.

Laprida 1214

I have ascended this staircase a now-secret-number of times. Xul-Solar used to wait for me above. This tall smiling man with high cheekbones combined Prussian, Slavic and Scandinavian blood (his father, Schulz, was from the Baltic). There was also Lombard and Latin blood (his mother was from the Italian north). More important was another conjunction: that of many languages and religions and, apparently, of all the stars, for he was an astrologer. People live, especially in Buenos Aires, passively accepting what is called reality.

Xul lived by re-forming and re-creating everything. He had contrived two jargons. One of them, his so-called *Creol,* was Spanish relieved of heavy ballast and enriched with unexpected neologisms. In the Spanish word for toy, *juguete,* he detected a malevolent *jugo* (juice); and he preferred to say *toybesan* ("toykiss") and *toyquieran* ("toylove"). He would ask others to "saintsitdown." And to an astonished Argentine lady, "I recommend the Tao to you," adding, "What, you don't cognizate the Tao Te Ching?" His other jargon was called *Panlanguage,* based on astrology. He had also invented *Panplay,* a kind of complex duodecimal chess which took place on a board boasting one hundred and forty-four squares. Every time he explained it to me he would decide it was too elementary, and would proceed to enrich it with new ramifications, with the result that I never learned it. We were in the habit of reading William Blake together, especially the Prophetic Books, whose mythology he would explain to me, although he was not always in accord with it. Xul admired Turner and Klee and he had the audacity, in the 1920s, not to admire Picasso. I suspect that he appreciated poetry less than language, and that for him the essentials were music and painting. He constructed a semicircular piano. Neither money nor success meant anything to him. Like Blake or Swedenborg, he lived in the realm of the spirits. He professed polytheism: a single God seemed to him too scant. He admired the Vatican as a solid Roman institution with branches in almost all of the cities of the atlas. I have never known a library more versatile and delectable than his. He introduced me to Deussen's *History of*

Philosophy, which does not begin, like the others, with Greece, but with India and China, and which devotes a chapter to Gilgamesh. He died on one of the Tigre Islands.

Xul had told his wife that he would not die so long as she held his hand. At the end of one night she had to leave him for a moment and, when she returned, Xul had died.

Every memorable man runs the risk of being minted in anecdotes. I make my contribution now toward accomplishing this inevitable destiny.

The Desert

A few hundred feet from the Pyramid, I bent down, scooped up a handful of sand and then, a little farther away, let it silently spill. Under my breath I said: *I am modifying the Sahara*. The deed was minimal, but the words, which were scarcely ingenious, were exact, and I considered that I had needed an entire life to say them. The memory of that moment is one of the most significant of my stay in Egypt.

Bradley believed that the present moment is the one in which the future, which flows toward us, disintegrates into the past; that is, being is a ceasing to be; or, as Boileau said, without melancholy:

Le moment où je parle est
déjà loin de moi.

Whatever the case, the eve of any endeavor, and a pregnant memory, are more real than the intangible present. The eve of a voyage is an integral part of the voyage itself.

Our trip to Europe began, in fact, the day before yesterday, August 22, but it was prefigured by a supper on the eighteenth. We gathered in a Japanese restaurant: María Kodama, Alberto Girri, Enrique Pezzoni and I. The food constituted an anthology of fugitive flavors from the Orient. The voyage, which seemed to us immediate, preexisted in the conversation and the unexpected champagne offered us by the woman who owned the restaurant. The singularity of Japanese premises on Piedad Street was augmented by a chorus of voices and music by some people from Nara or Kamakura, who were celebrating a birthday. We were in Buenos Aires, on the threshold of a voyage to Europe, and at the same time in a Japan of memory and premonition. I shall not forget that night.

Staubbach

Much less famous than Niagara Falls but far more imposing and memorable is the *Staubbach* of Lauterbrunnen, the Dust Stream of the Clear Fountains. It was revealed to me around 1916. I heard, from far away, the deep murmur of the heavy vertical water breaking from a great height into a stone well which it endlessly carves and deepens, as it has from near the beginning of time. We spent a night there. For us, as for the people in the village, the constant roar became, in the end, confused with silence.

There are so many things in multiple Switzerland: there is also a place for the awesome.

Colonia del Sacramento

They have known war here, too. I say "too" because the description would fit almost any place on earth. The killing of man by man is one of the most ancient habits of our singular species, like procreation or dreams. Here, from the other side of the sea, stretched the vast shade of Aljubarrota and of those kings who are now dust. There was warfare here between Castilians and Portuguese, who later assumed other names. I know that one of my ancestors took part in the siege of this garrison during the Brazil War.

Here we feel the unequivocal presence of time, so rare in these latitudes. These walls and houses contain the past, and that is a savor to be appreciated in America. Names and dates are unnecessary. What we immediately feel is enough, as if we were listening to music.

La Recoleta Cemetery in Buenos Aires

Here lies: not Isidoro Suárez, who led the charge of the hussars at the battle of Junín, which was scarcely a skirmish and which changed the history of America.

Here lies: not Félix Olavarría, who shared with Suárez the campaigns, the conspiracy, the long marches, the high snow, the risks, the friendship and exile. Here lies the dust of his dust.

Here lies: not my grandfather, who got himself killed after Mitre's surrender at La Verde.

Here lies: not my father, who taught me to disbelieve in intolerable immortality.

Here lies: not my mother, who forgave me too many things.

Here, beneath the epitaphs and the crosses, there is almost nothing.

I will not lie here. My hair and my nails will lie here, and they will not know that the rest is gone and they will go on growing and will become dust.

I will not lie here, but will be part of oblivion, the tenuous substance of which the universe is made.

On Salvation by Deeds

One autumn, one of the autumns of time, the Shinto divinities gathered, not for the first time, at Izumo. They are said to have numbered eight million. Being a shy man I would have felt a bit lost among so many. In any case, it is not convenient to deal in inconceivable numbers. Let us say there were eight, since eight is a good omen in these islands.

They were downcast, but did not show it: the visages of divinities are undecipherable kanji. They seated themselves in a circle on the green crest of a hill. They had been observing mankind from their firmament or from a stone or from a snowflake. One of the divinities spoke:

Many days, or centuries, ago, we gathered here to create Japan and the world. The fishes, the seas, the seven colors of the rainbow, the generations of plants and animals have all worked out well. So that men should not be burdened with too many things, we gave them succession, issue, the plural day and the singular night. We also bestowed on them the gift of experimenting with certain variations. The bee continues repeating beehives. But man has imagined devices: the plow, the key, the kaleidoscope. He also imagined the sword and

the art of war. He has just imagined an invisible weapon which could put an end to history. Before this senseless deed is done, let us wipe out men.

They remained pensive. Without haste another divinity spoke:

It's true. They have thought up that atrocity, but there is also this something quite different, which fits in the space encompassed by seventeen syllables.

The divinity intoned them. They were in an unknown language, and I could not understand them.

The leading divinity delivered a judgment:

Let men survive.

Thus, because of a *haiku,* the human race was saved.

Izumo, April 27, 1984.

Notes

p. 12: "Retiro": A railway station and park in the northern section of Buenos Aires. El Retiro means The Retreat.

p. 26: "Bollini's Alley": A street in Buenos Aires.

p. 43: "whose name I can no longer recall": An allusion to the opening of *Don Quixote* by Cervantes.

"a button": A large, white-painted aluminum sculpture, some eighteen feet in diameter, placed in front of the Van Pelt Library on the University of Pennsylvania campus in Philadelphia. It was installed in the summer of 1981 at a cost of $100,000, funded by the National Endowment for the Arts and other donors; the upper part is four feet higher than the lower part, representing a break in the button. The piece is the work of Claes Oldenburg (b. 1929), Swedish-born American sculptor who usually uses "soft" (vinyl and foam rubber) materials; a fomenter of the Pop Art movement in the U.S. and Europe.

p. 47: "Montaner y Simón": Catalan publishing house.

p. 56: "Rosas": Juan Manuel de Rosas (1793–1877), Argentine *caudillo,* large landowner, strongman and tyrant. He died in exile in England, where he had lived for twenty-five years.

"Once": A section in the west of Buenos Aires.

"Macedonio Fernández": Argentine writer, philosopher, wit (1874–1952), an eccentric voice in Borges' memories. Borges is "always coming back to Macedonio." Borges judged him "the most admirable conversationalist I've ever known," but he wrote "a sort of almost unreadable baroque style." Typical of Borges' quotations from Macedonio's conversation is the aphorism: "Historians are as knowledgeable about the past as we are ignorant about the present."

"Léon Bloy": French Catholic writer (1846–1917), a fervent convert, spiritual mentor to the novelist Huysmans, the philosopher Jacques Maritain and the painter Georges Rouault. In early writings, Borges concluded that Bloy, despite his inspired and imaginative Catholicism, was, like Blake or Swedenborg, actually a heresiarch.

"Leandro Alem": Argentine politician (1842–1896), founder of the Unión Cívica Radical, a populist political party. He committed suicide with a pistol in his carriage. Early on, Borges was "a Radical, simply because my grandfather . . . was a close friend of Alem." He soon found he was a "natural conservative," and joined the Conservative Party. When it was pointed out that the party could not win an election, Borges answered in words he later made famous in "The Form of the Sword": "Only lost causes can interest a gentleman."

"Estanislao del Campo": Argentine writer (1834–1880), a city-man who wrote country poetry in "gaucho style"; best known for *Fausto* (1866), a parody of Gounod's and Goethe's work, a parody which Lugones called "an intrinsically transient and vile genre." Paul Groussac called Campo "a law-office gaucho troubador." But Borges has pointed out that Estanislao del Campo "was a cavalry officer and the cavalry was made up of gauchos." At that time, Borges adds, it was hard "to know people who were *not* gauchos." Argentina was in fact "a nation of gauchos" in the 1860s.

p. 58: "Brennus": Chieftain in Gaul who invaded Italy in 390 B.C.

Vae Victis!: "Woe to the Vanquished!"

p. 64: "a river so slow that literature has called it immobile." An allusion to the title of a novel by Eduardo Mallea (1903–1983), *La Cuidad junto al rio immóvil,* Buenos Aires, 1938.

"Leopoldo Lugones": Leading Argentine poet and writer (1874–1938). "Lugones—if we accept his baroque style— was a great writer," according to Borges, who published a small book and conducted seminars on him.

"El Tigre": An archipelago of hundreds of islands to the northwest of Buenos Aires.

p. 65: Milonga: An Argentine ballroom dance which preceded the tango in the early twentieth century; musicologists associate it with the gauchos.

"Pehuajó": A town in the Province of Buenos Aires.

p. 70: "Ars Magna": *Ars generalis ultima,* the final summation (including the *Arbor scientiae* and the *Liber de ascensu et descensu intellectus,* (1305–8), of the "combinatory arts" of Raymundo Lulio (Llull); see below.

"Raymundo (Ramón or Raimundo) Lulio": Original Catalan Raymond (or Raymund) Llull, called in English Lully (1234–1316); Mallorcan mystic and poet who strove to encompass all knowledge in convergent points of unity. He wrote in Latin, Arabic and Catalan; author of the *Ars magna;* "the 'Art' remained influential until long after the Renaissance, ultimately inspiring Leibniz's dream of a 'universal algebra.' " (R.D.F. Pring-Mill, *Encyclopaedia Britannica,* Chicago, London, 1973, Vol. 14, p. 172.)

p. 72: "Mauthner": Fritz Mauthner (1849–1923), German author and exponent of philosophical skepticism who believed that words belie reality; were good for poetry but not thinking, and that only experience shaped by cultural influences leads to truth. Borges has said: Mauthner "was a Jew of Czech origin. . . . He published some very bad novels, but his philosophical papers are excellent."

p. 73: "Lavardén": Manuel José de Lavardén (1754–1809), Argentine poet who composed an ode to the River Plate.

"Manrique": Jorge Manrique (1440–1479), Spanish poet in whose famous *Coplas* (written on the death of his father—the Grand Master Don Rodrigo—and admirably translated by Longfellow) human lives are compared to rivers running to the sea.

p. 74: "Junín": The first of two decisive battles in the South American war of nationalist independence against imperial Spain in 1824. In Peru.

"Artigas": José Gervasio Artigas (1764–1850), Uruguayan *caudillo* and leader in the battle for nationalist independence.

"Solano López": Francisco Solano López (1826–1870), *caudillo* and leader of Paraguay.

p. 77: "Xul-Solar": Alejandro Schulz (Oscar Agustín Alejandro Schulz Solari); "Xul" was his version of Schulz and "Solar" of Solari (1887–1963), Argentine mystic, painter, eccentric, neo-linguist, "local metaphysician." He illustrated three books by Borges; five of the nineteen items in the bibliography of "Pierre Menard, Author of Don Quixote" reflect Xul's interests. In "An Autobiographical Essay," Borges wrote: "In a rough and ready way . . . Xul, who was a mystic poet and painter, is our William Blake."

p. 83: "Bradley": F. H. Bradley (1846–1924), English philosopher of the absolute idealist school; his position approached that of a "feeling" solipsism. T. S. Eliot wrote his Harvard doctoral dissertation in philosophy on Bradley (1916) and it later became a book.

p. 84: "Le moment où je parle est/déjà loin de moi.": The moment in which I speak is already far from me.

p. 86: "Colonia del Sacramento": A military outpost of the Portuguese Colonialists (and later their descendants, the Brazilians), founded on the banks of the River Plate in the late seventeenth century, in what is now Uruguay. For a century and a half it came under intermittent siege from Spanish (i.e. Castilian) settlers and their descendants (i.e. Uruguayans and Argentines) until it finally passed into Spanish hands in 1828, during the Brazil War. Borges sets this piece of history against the much earlier victory of the Portuguese over the Castilians at Aljubarrota in 1385, a battle that secured their independence from Spanish kings.

p. 88: "Mitre's surrender at La Verde": Bartolomé Mitre (1821–1906), statesman, soldier, author and translator (of Dante and others); President of Argentina, 1862–68. Mitre was defeated by Sarmiento during the revolutionary uprising of 1874. Borges' grandfather fought on Mitre's side, and was mortally wounded a few minutes *after* Mitre's surrender.